DATE DUE			
JUL 6 2001			
JUL 9 5			

The Bird Fisherman

Nicole Schneegans was born in Randan (Puy-de-Dome), France. Married with three children, she is the editor-in-chief of the magazine, Lire au collége, and author of many novels. Her work has been published by Nathan, Flammarion, Stock, Cerf, and Amitié.

Jean Claverie was born in Beaune in 1948. Trained at the École des arts décoratifs in Geneva, he now splits his time between teaching and illustrating children's books. Published by Gallimard, Albin Michel and Centurion, his works have won him many prizes and awards, one of which was the graphic award from Loisirs jeunes in 1981.

The Bird Fisherman

A story written by Nicole Schneegans
illustrated by Jean Claverie

THE CHILD'S WORLD
MANKATO, MINNESOTA

I Can Fly

I'm nine years old and I happen to be an unusual guy. For example, when my dad gives me some money and asks me to get him a bag of candy, I fly.

Yes, I fly to the newstand owned by Mrs. Champ. It's about five minutes away from my house, on the same side of the street.

In my neighborhood, all the houses are right next to each other. However, every so often there is a break in the sidewalk about a yard or two wide, sometimes even more.

So when I go out our door, then out of the gate of our yard, I take off. It's easy. At the end of the first section of sidewalk, I'm running so fast that my right leg goes up all by itself! I fly over the break and then plop! I land on both legs at the edge of the next part of the sidewalk. I keep doing this all the way to Mrs. Champ's store.

With the change from the bag of candy, I buy some caramels and a pack of gum. What I really like is to try to jump and stay up in the air for as long as possible.

It's all I think about! I know all cracks in all the sidewalks all the way up my street. I especially like the ones between my house and Mrs. Champ's store. On these, I'm incredible! After each trip to buy candy, I can stay in the air longer and longer. I

should tell you something, though, one reason I'm getting so much better is because I practice so much at night, in my dreams.

In my dreams, it's amazing. In one flying leap, I cover the whole street, all the way to the football field. It's a great feeling. It feels as if flying is something so natural that we all know how to do it. When I fly in my dreams, Superman is like a shakey duck next to me!

You might not believe me, but yesterday something very strange happened to me.

I jumped up into the air with so much speed that instead of coming down on both

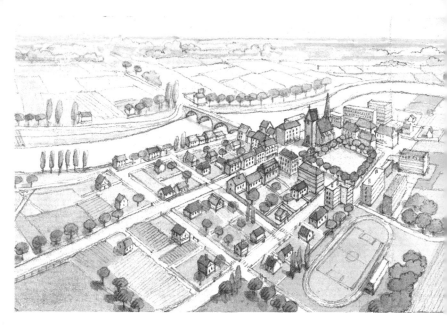

legs in front of Mrs. Champ's store, I kept going up into the air! My leaps were getting so high that I was jumping over two or three sidewalk sections at a time. When I landed on the ground, I barely grazed it, then I was off, jumping even higher.

Going along like this, I went right past my street and off toward the Blue Forest. In this forest, the trees are so thick that I was afraid of getting stuck in the branches if I came down. Not a single clearing in sight.

So, not only did I stay up in the air, but I climbed higher and higher. I didn't stop going up until I was right up in the middle of the sky.

I had to take a rest. There was a little cloud that looked quite comfortable to me. I curled up into a ball as I went over it, then gently, I fell down onto it.

I Find a Friend

Then everything happened like in a mattress ad on television. I bounced up and down two or three times because it was so soft, then I settled into the middle of the cloud.

The blue sky all around me looked like the sea. The forest and the town below me were the shore. I felt like I was on an island of whipped cream. It was hot. I was sure going to get a good tan. Anyway, I was moving along.

My cloud was lower than most of the

other clouds and it scooted along quickly. To help it along, I lay down on my stomach and paddled. As they passed by, migrating birds looked at me in amazement.

The sky is not as empty as it seems. It's crazy all the things you run into up there! Aside from a flock of swallows, a pack of wild ducks, and a slew of sparrows, I saw a good half dozen different kinds of airplanes.

But the weirdest thing that I discovered on this strange flight of mine was the bird fisherman. I didn't even know that there

was such a thing as a bird fisherman! I guess that this kind of job is headed toward extinction.

The gentleman passed me on a cloud a little bit bigger than mine. He didn't see me because he was watching his hook. He seemed very preoccupied.

However, what he was doing wasn't really that unusual. The bird fisherman was sitting on the edge of his cloud. He held a cane fishing pole out into the sky. On the fish hook was wiggling some kind of

creature that could have been a worm, I wasn't quite sure. The migrating birds would try to swallow it and then they'd get caught.

When we were right next to each other, the bird fisherman caught a lark.

I yelled out, "Are they biting today?"

The fisherman sat still, completely

surprised, then he lifted up his eyes and saw me. He quickly unhooked the bird, threw his fishing line in my direction and hooked the cloud I was on. I was being pulled in toward him.

He said to me, "All right now, what are you doing up here?"

I answered dumbly, "I'm just hanging around, and you?"

"I'm getting my dinner. Come on over, but be careful when you jump."

I gathered in energy, like I did before jumping from the fourth to the fifth piece of sidewalk near Mrs. Champ's, and I landed right next to him.

A Picnic on a Cloud

He was a funny old guy. He wore a large hat made of feathers and overalls with different colored patches. He didn't wear shoes, but on the end of his socks were two long wool cords, each with a pompom on the end.

We talked about this and that. I told him that I wasn't really there on purpose and I was sorry if I was bothering him. Actually he seemed happy to have a visitor, because he told me, "Kid, you have the gift of flight. It's so old and so rare that it's been forgotten. Now, everyone tries so hard to

make airplanes instead of just remembering what we were once able to do."

I was only half listening to him because what kept catching my eye were those pompoms. I couldn't take my eyes off of them while he was making us something to eat.

In his left hand, the lark was wiggling. He took a mirror out of his pocket and with a single ray of the sun, he killed the lark cleanly. Maybe it was because I was afraid

to watch it die that I kept looking at the feet of the fisherman. He finally noticed.

"You looking at my pompoms? You want to know what I use them for? OK, it's like this. When I lay down to sleep, I let them dangle over the edge. The wind makes them spin around and they chase away the flies."

"Flies? Up this high?"

"Kind of. They aren't the same flies that you have down below. But, you know, the air is full of all sorts of flying insects, especially at night. I'm up here to take life easy, so I chase them away. When you think about it, I have a dream life."

Suddenly, I had a strange idea and I asked, "Are you really here or are you in a dream that I'm having?"

"Don't think about that. Look, see how

the sun has cooked our lark. We'll share it!"

The roast lark was wonderful, I tell you! When I was thirsty, the bird fisherman got me a large drink of rainwater in an eagle's skull. To get it for me, all he had to do was take a corner of the cloud in his hands and

wring it. When he saw how surprised I
was, he started laughing. Then, looking
around, he said, "If you're really thirsty,
we can take your cloud and squeeze it dry.
You really don't need it anymore."

I felt a little uneasy about that, "Well, it's

21

just that, Mr. Bird Fisherman, when I want to go, I'm going to need my cloud!"

"Go away! You're all alike! Kid, you are so lucky to be able to fly. And you're so lucky that you met me, the last bird fisherman, and you're already talking about leaving. Besides, there are so many amazing things in the sky!"

"Yes, I've seen them - hundreds of birds, wonderful clouds, airplanes... and I've met you too!"

"Oh, but that's not all. I'm going to tell you a secret. I'm going to tell you simply because you seem so nice. But it's a secret! Can you be trusted?"

"You could cut me into little pieces before I'd tell a secret!"

"Ok, promise and cross your heart."

I crossed my heart right there, standing on the cloud. The bird fisherman shook my hand and looked me straight in the eye.

I Meet a Rare Bird

We were sitting comfortably on the white fluffy cloud.

"O.K. kid, you know that my job is to fish for birds, but only for eating. I have discovered a bird that is not like the others. This one I don't try to catch, because it is like me, the last of its kind."

"It's the only bird like it?"

"Absolutely. None other. I call it 'the rare bird.' I don't think that anyone else has ever seen it. Because you can fly, I want to show it to you."

"Oh! That would be great! Can we go see

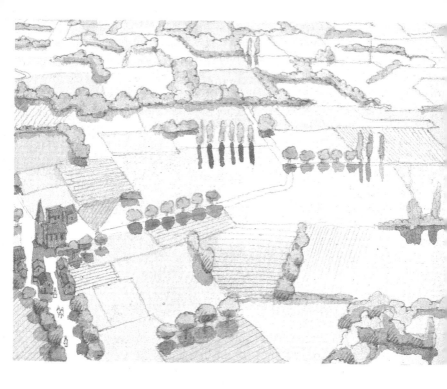

it right now? I promise I won't tell anyone."

The bird fisherman stood up straight and tall and he became very serious. "I have to warn you, kid, that this could be very dangerous. This bird lives in the wind and storm zone. Get ready and do everything that I tell you."

So we got ready to go. To make it easier to move around, I jumped back onto my cloud which was still hooked up to the

other one. I lay on my stomach and tried to paddle exactly like the bird fisherman did. We whipped across the sky. Underneath us, I could see the clouds, towns and towers go by. I was a little nervous that we were getting so far away from my town.

From time to time, the fisherman would turn and wave at me. I would wave back and try not to wiggle too much. The weather was turning bad. It was gray all around us.

The wind was picking up.

My friend yelled, "Hook up to me! We're almost there. I'll start to descend into the forest. Right down there is where the rare bird lives."

I was so afraid that I wished I was standing on my two feet in front of Mrs. Champ's store. The turbulence was terrible. I couldn't tell if we were going down or if the forest was rising. I felt sick to my stomach. Finally we slowed down.

"Here we are!" the fisherman yelled to me.

We stopped right in a patch of fog.

Then I heard an odd call, but it didn't come from the sky. It was the fisherman

who made this sound by cupping his hands around his mouth.

Suddenly, a similar call answered. Leaning on my elbows, I saw an enormous bird of every color appear. It shone like the sun in the middle of the fog. It was the rare bird. It flew around us, singing the whole time. The fisherman and the bird

understood each other, that was for sure.

At the same time, my friend took some seeds out of his pocket. He threw them up into the sky. The bird caught them. It  soared, turned and came back. Soon the songs of the fisherman and the bird became softer, slower, like a farewell song. It was then that I became aware of

something horrible. Huge holes were appearing in the middle of our clouds. I grabbed all that was left of my cloud and held on to it.

The fisherman panicked, "Watch out, kid! We're too low. Paddle as hard as you can or we're going to crash!"

I Was Afraid!

I tried as hard as I could to do like the fisherman.

He was paddling carefully. At the same time, he started to sing again. This time, he was calling for help! The bird answered by flying close to us. With its huge wings, it batted the air, flying in circles around our clouds. It helped. We were no longer getting sucked down. The wind that the bird created helped us gently ascend and little by little, our clouds got fuller and thicker.

We were still in danger, because as soon as the bird flew away, everything started to fall apart again.

"Get off your cloud!" yelled the fisherman. "Jump to mine. That will be easier."

Between his cloud and mine, there wasn't any more distance than between the fourth and fifth piece of sidewalk in front of Mrs.

Champ's. So I jumped! But at that very moment, a gust of wind broke up the fisherman's cloud. I felt myself falling into nothing! But not for long, because the bird had seen me.

Just as I thought I was going to die, I found myself astride his back, my fingers gripping the feathers of his wings.

"Saved!" shouted the fisherman. Then he began to whistle to the bird again.

The bird turned toward the fisherman. I wondered how I was going to join my friend, because his cloud was still too soft for the bird to land on.

Then I had an idea.

"Mr. Fisherman! I'm going to grab on to your pompoms and climb up to you!"

He nodded his head "yes" and then whistled to the bird.

The bird, slowly flapping his wings, went right under the fisherman, but he couldn't stop. I held up my hands. On the first try, I didn't catch them. Second try, reaching up higher, I caught them. O.K. I swung for a moment or two at the end of the fisherman's stockings, hoping that they didn't come off his feet!

Very quickly, my friend caught me under the arms and pulled me up to him. I finally took a deep breath!

For quite a while the bird flew around us, until finally we found a good air current and we picked up our normal speed.

"Oof!" the fisherman said to me. "This time, we made it!"

He took out of his pocket another handful of seeds that he threw up into the air. After that the bird flew away singing, the song slowly fading away. Soon it had disappeared into the fog.

The fisherman asked me, "Weren't you afraid?"

"Yes, I was. But it was worth it. Just think about it - I was saved by the rare

bird. Hey, I know, Mr. Bird Fisherman, to celebrate the event, do you want a caramel? I have one in my pocket."

The fisherman shook his head sadly, "You know, if I eat a caramel, then I'll just want another and another... I would prefer not to start, so keep it for yourself!"

As for me, all emotions make me hungry. While eating my caramel, I asked him some

questions, "Really, you never get bored staying up here all by yourself in the sky?"

"Once I had a wife, but she died. And my two sons... One after the other, they wanted to go down to the town. After awhile they forgot how to fly. Say, kid, would you like to stay up here with me?"

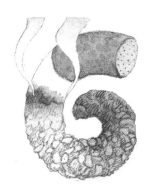

I'll Come Back!

I didn't know what to say. I didn't think I could really live in the sky.

But the fisherman insisted, "At first, I'll tow you and I'll teach you the job. We can stay over your town so that you feel more at home. Little by little, you can go off on your own..."

As he was saying this to me, we floated over my town. Even in the distance, I could make out the big street and the chimney of our house. By this time, Dad was probably getting mad because he was out of candy and I hadn't come back.

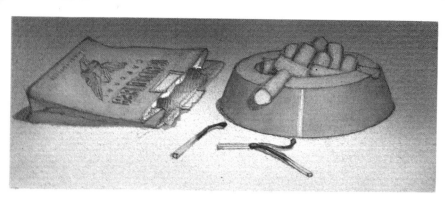

I hated to make anyone feel bad so I was in a tough spot! I tried to think of a way out and suddenly the bird fisherman said, "Listen, I will take that caramel."

Just as I handed him one of the remaining caramels, I figured out what to do, "Hey, I have an idea! Really, I'd like to stay with you and become a bird fisherman, but the thing that I love the most in life is to jump high, really high, and stay up a long time, and then land on my feet in front of Mrs. Champ's store. Mrs. Champ sells everything - caramels, gum, candy bars, Twinkies, mints, really, she sells everything. So this is what I'd like to do - since I know how to fly, I'll come up and see you regularly and I'll bring you anything you want."

The fisherman's eyes lit up at the idea.

"You will come and see me? Every week, by jumping, by flying? You will come however you come?"

"It's a promise. And I won't come empty handed."

"You'll tell·me what's going on down below?"

"I'll even bring you the paper if you'd like. I'll come like I did today. I'll start

running by my house. I'll skim over the sidewalk. I'll jump over the football field. I'll climb over the forest and there I'll be! I can come every Wednesday around two o'clock."

"Perfect, that'll be terrific! Shake on it! I'm very happy. Now, it's getting late. I'll help you get down. Maybe some day you'll decide to stay up here and then you'll be the last bird fisherman."

After that, I can't exactly tell you how I found myself standing in front of Mrs.

Champ's store, on my two feet, and with the money in my hand. Things just happened too fast, kind of like a dream, you might say.

Anyway, next Wednesday, I'm going back up to the sky.

English edition copyright © 1993 by The Child's World, Inc.
123 South Broad Street, Mankato, Minnesota 56001
French edition copyright © 1990 Bayard Presse

Library of Congress Cataloging-in-Publication Data

Schneegans, Nicole, 1941-
    The bird fisherman / written by Nicole Schneegans: illustrated by Jean
Claverie. p. cm.
    Summary: A nine-year-old boy who has discovered how to fly journeys
up into the clouds and meets the bird fisherman, an unusual gentleman who
fishes for birds.
    ISBN 0-89565-896-8
    [1. Flight – Fiction.]   I. Claverie, Jean, 1946- ill.   II. Title.
PZ7.S3615Bi   1992
[Fic] – dc20   91-45926
                                                                 CIP
                                                                 AC